Dear God, are You still awake?
Have You got a minute or two?
You're pretty good at understanding,
And I really need to talk to You.

You see, Mommy came to tuck me in,
Like she does every night.
I was trying to play a trick on her,
Since she can't see without the light.

I was going to close my eyes
And pretend to be asleep.
But when I heard her crying,
I didn't dare let out a peep.

She started talking to You, God.
Did You hear the things she said?
Could You hear what she was saying
As she stood beside my bed?

Why would Mommy be so sad?
I wondered just what I had done,
And then I began to remember it all
As she named them one by one...

This morning we worked in the garden,
But, honest, I really didn't know
That if I picked all those little yellow blooms
The tomatoes wouldn't grow!

Charlie and I were trying to be helpers,
'Cause I know that's what Mommy needs,
But I don't think she was too happy with us
When we pulled up carrots instead of weeds.

Mommy said we should stop for the day,
She decided we had helped quite enough.
I sure had worked up an appetite...
I didn't know gardening was so tough!

We had peanut-butter and jelly for lunch,
And I shared too much, I guess...
But I didn't realize until I was done
That Charlie had made such a mess.

Mommy said she needed a nap,
She had one of her headaches today.
She told me to keep an eye on my sister
And find something quiet to play.

Well, God, do You remember all those curls
You gave my little sister Jenny?
We played barber shop...very quietly...
And now, well, she doesn't have any.

Boy, was Mommy mad at me...
I had to go sit on my bed.
She said never to cut "people hair" again.
I guess I'll practice on Charlie instead.

We sat and watched poor old Albert,
I just knew he must be so bored
Going round and round in the same place all day,
Wouldn't You think so, Lord?

I didn't think it would hurt to let him out for awhile.
I mean, mice need exercise, too.
By the way, have You seen Albert lately?
He's been sort of missing since two.

Mommy sent us outside for the rest of the day.
She said we needed fresh air.
But when Daddy came home she told him
She was trying to get something out of her hair.

We thought Mommy needed cheering up,
So we decided to brighten her day.
But, God, did You see the look on her face
When we gave her that pretty bouquet?

We had gotten a little bit dirty,
So Mommy said to get in the tub.
"Use soap this time," she reminded,
"And please don't forget to scrub."

Charlie didn't like the water too much,
But I lathered up real good.
I knew Mommy would be so proud of me
For cleaning up like I should.

I went downstairs to the table,
But during dinner it started to rain...
I'd forgotten to turn off the water, it seems,
And I hadn't unplugged the drain!

I decided right then it was just about time
To start getting ready for bed,
When Mommy said, "It's sure been a long day,"
And her face began turning all red.

I lay there listening to Mommy
As she told You about our day.
I thought about all of the things I had done
And I wondered what I should say.

I was just about to tell her
That I'd been awake all along,
And ask her to please forgive me
For all of those things I'd done wrong.

When suddenly, I heard her whisper,
"God, forgive me for today...
For not being more understanding
When those problems came my way...

For not handling situations
In the way You wanted me to...
For getting angry and losing my temper,
Things I know You don't want me to do.

And, God, please give me more patience,
Help me make it through another day,
I'll do better tomorrow, I promise...
In Jesus' name I pray."

Wiping her eyes, she kissed me
And knelt here beside my bed.
She stroked my hair for a little while...
"I love you, precious," Mommy said.

She left the room without ever knowing
That I'd been awake all the time.
And God, could we make it our little secret?
You know, just Yours and mine?

I'm sorry I was so much trouble today,
I really didn't mean to be...
Daddy says it's tough being a kid sometimes,
But I think it's harder on Mommy than me.

Well, goodnight, God. Thanks for listening.
It's sure nice to know You're there.
I feel so much better when I talk to You
'Cause You always hear my prayer.

And I'll do better tomorrow, I promise...
Just You wait and see!
I'll try not to be so much trouble again,
But, God, please give more patience to Mommy...

...Just in case!

Amen.